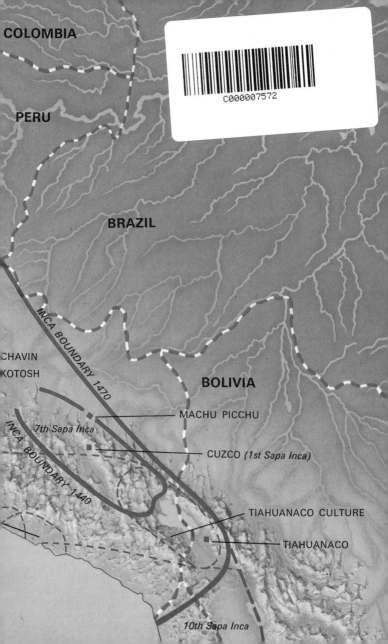

*How to pronounce some of the difficult words in this book :*

| | |
|---|---|
| amautas | *am-ow-tass* |
| Atahualpa | *Atta-wal-pa* |
| Cajamarca | *Ka-ha-marr-ka* |
| chasqui | *chass-kee* |
| conquistadors | *kon-kist-a-doors* |
| Coricancha | *Korri-kancha* |
| Ecuador | *Eck-wa-door* |
| Hatun Uillca | *Hat-oon-wilca* |
| Huascar | *Hwass-car* |
| Huayna Capac | *Hwyna-Kapak* |
| Illapa | *Ill-a-pa* |
| Inti Raymi | *Inti Rymi* |
| Mama-Quilla | *Mamma Kilia* |
| Orejones | *Orr-e-hon-ess* |
| Pachacuti | *Patch-a-cooti* |
| Quechua | *Kechwa* |
| Quito | *Keeto* |
| San Miguel | *San Mee-gell* |
| Tahuantinsuyu | *Ta-wan-tin-soo-yoo* |
| Tupac Inca Yupanqui | *Toopak Inca Yoo-pan-kee* |
| Villac Uma | *Veelak Ooma* |
| Viracocha | *Virra-kocha* |
| Xuaca | *Wa-ka* |
| Yana Uillca | *Yanna Wilca* |

*Acknowledgment:* The photographs on page 32 and pages 50-51 are reproduced by permission of Mrs Sarah Cotton.

*Great Civilisations*
# The Incas

by BRENDA RALPH LEWIS
with illustrations by JORGE NUÑEZ

Ladybird Books  Loughborough

Francisco Pizarro felt sick and dizzy and his head ached. The Spaniards with him (there were nearly two hundred of them) all felt just as bad. They were suffering from the effects of the high altitude in the great Andes mountains of Peru. The Spaniards struggled along the rough mountain paths, shivering despite their heavy armour in the cold mountain wind.

Pizarro shielded his eyes and gazed at the scene in front of him. There was nothing but mountains to be

seen. Some of the most gigantic ones were over 20,000 feet (6000 m) high and their peaks and upper slopes were cloaked in thick snow that never melted.

In between the mountains were deep gorges where the air was so hot and sticky that it was difficult to move or breathe. Here and there, there were fresh green valleys, where Pizarro's men and horses could rest for a while, but there were not many of them. Most of the country was harsh, empty and lonely.

'We could all die here and no one would ever find us!' Pizarro murmured gloomily to himself. Then he smiled. An important word had just come into his mind, a word that had inspired him to lead his expedition into the mountains of Peru in the autumn of 1532. The word was *gold*. Gold! Enough, Pizarro reflected, to satisfy even the greediest of men!

*Cuzco, the Inca capital*

Pizarro and his Spaniards were indeed greedy men. Peru offered a great deal to be greedy about, for it seemed to be full of precious metals. The inhabitants of Peru, the Incas, had so much gold and silver that they made food bowls and drinking cups out of them. They piled golden ornaments inside their temples and hung them on the walls.

The Sapa Inca, the ruler of the Inca Empire, had golden walls in the rooms of his palaces. Pizarro had even heard of statues and models of people and animals made of pure gold, and of ornamental trees bearing gold and silver 'fruit'.

The buildings in Cuzco, the Inca capital, had roofs made of gold, and walls decorated with golden tapestries.

'This whole country is one great treasure-house!' Pizarro thought.

Despite his painful headache, Pizarro felt very happy. All the dangers he and his men were facing on their 200-mile (330 km) trek from San Miguel to Cajamarca were well worthwhile.

When Pizarro met the Sapa Inca, Atahualpa, in Cajamarca, he was going to demand that Atahualpa become a Christian and hand over his wealthy empire to King Charles of Spain. Pizarro was not worried that Atahualpa would refuse these demands, for the Inca ruler seemed to be quite excited at the approaching arrival of the Spaniards. He had even sent a *chasqui* (runner) to Pizarro with a gift of a pair of painted shoes and some gold bracelets.

*A winged god in gold and turquoise forms the handle of a ceremonial knife*

It may seem strange that Atahualpa felt so friendly towards the Spaniards who had come into his empire; these greedy, grasping men were, after all, more interested in Atahualpa's treasure than in his friendship.

Atahualpa did not know this, though. Because Pizarro came from over the sea, and had a beard, the Sapa Inca thought that he was the great bearded Inca god Viracocha. (The Incas were a smooth-skinned people and beards were very unusual.) He also thought that Pizarro's men were Viracocha's attendants, the demi-gods.

The Incas worshipped Viracocha as the creator of the world. An old prophecy had forecast that he would one day return to Peru by sea. The Spaniards had come to Peru by sea, from Panama. So you can see how this case of mistaken identity arose.

However, if the Inca ruler did not know the truth about the Spaniards, neither did the Spaniards know much about the Incas or about their empire. It was completely strange to them, quite different from Spain and Europe and from the life people lived there.

*One of Pizarro's caravels*
*sailing from Panama*

9

For one thing, Atahualpa was a much more powerful ruler than the Spaniards' king, Charles. King Charles was honoured and respected by his subjects, of course, but he was not regarded as a god. Atahualpa was. Just look at the titles by which he was known. He was the Sapa Inca (usually translated as Supreme Inca), Lord of the World, Son of the Sun and god. Atahualpa was thought to be so great and grand that no one was good enough to eat with him, so he ate alone. Twice a day, gold and silver dishes were set out before him on a fine cotton cloth or a mat of woven reeds laid on the floor. The dishes contained foods like llama meat, duck, fish, vegetables and fruit. From these dishes, Atahualpa chose the ones he wanted. A handmaiden stood by holding a lump of rock salt in case Atahualpa wanted to lick it and so make his meal more spicy.

Atahualpa was the thirteenth Sapa Inca of Tahuantinsuyu, which was the Incas' name for the Empire of Peru (it meant 'land of the four provinces'). Tahuantinsuyu contained about six million people and extended over an area of 380,000 square miles (990,000 sq km), from present-day Ecuador through Peru all the way down to central Chile.

Tahuantinsuyu had not always been as large as this. In about 1200 A D, at the time of the first Sapa Inca, Manco Capac, the Incas had been only a small tribe living in and around the town of Cuzco.

It seems that this situation did not change very much until after 1438, when the ninth Sapa Inca, Pachacuti, came to the throne. Pachacuti made war against neighbouring tribes and conquered them, one after the other. The ninth Sapa Inca was a very old man, probably over eighty when he abdicated in 1471 and gave his throne to his son, Tupac Inca Yupanqui. Tupac now became the tenth Sapa Inca and carried on his father's work. Pachacuti had conquered the tribes in the north as far as Quito in Ecuador. Tupac Inca Yupanqui overcame the peoples in the south, all the way down to the Maule river in Chile. That left unconquered only the tribes who lived round what is now the border between Ecuador and Colombia. These were overcome by Tupac's son and successor, Huayna Capac, who became Sapa Inca in 1493.

Atahualpa, who was born in about 1502, was one of Huayna Capac's sons. He was not the heir to the throne, though: that position was held by Atahualpa's elder half-brother Huascar. Even so, Atahualpa seems to have been Huayna Capac's favourite. In 1513, when Atahualpa was about eleven, Huayna Capac took the boy with him when he went to war against rebels in and around Quito. Huayna Capac defeated the rebels and it is thought that he decreed that after his death, Atahualpa would rule Quito province.

Huayna Capac may not have realised how much trouble his decree would one day cause. What worried him more were the reports about the arrival of white-skinned strangers in Peru, which reached him in 1524. These strangers were *conquistadors* (Spanish conquerors), who were exploring the Pacific coast of the Inca Empire: one of them was Francisco Pizarro.

To increase Huayna Capac's fears, Peru suffered violent earthquakes and huge tidal waves swept away Inca villages along the Pacific coast. One night, the trembling Incas saw that the Moon had three rings around it; one was the colour of blood. Huayna Capac, like his subjects, was extremely superstitious and he was terrified when the *amautas* (wise men) told him that the Moon's three rings foretold the coming of plague, war and destruction for the Inca people.

Of these disasters, the plague came first. It took the form of a frightful epidemic (probably smallpox), which the Spaniards brought with them from Europe. Thousands of Incas caught it and a great many of them died. One of the first epidemic victims was Huayna Capac himself. Some time between 1525 and 1527, he fell ill at his palace in Quito and died there soon after-

*Pizarro at the court of King Charles of Spain*

wards. Atahualpa, who was with his father in Quito, sent a chasqui to the Inca capital at Cuzco to tell Huascar what had happened. Later, Atahualpa seized hold of Huayna Capac's treasure and took control of his army.

Huascar was furious when he learned what Atahualpa had done. Huascar had never liked the idea of his ambitious half-brother ruling Quito province and so becoming a rival to him. So Huascar demanded that Atahualpa come to Cuzco and hand Quito over to him, together with Huayna Capac's army. If Atahualpa failed to obey then, Huascar threatened, he would attack him. That of course meant *civil war* (fighting between two groups in the same country).

Atahualpa had no intention of doing what his half-brother demanded, nor did he wait for Huascar to attack. Instead he gathered his army and marched southwards from Quito province. Soon afterwards, there took place the first of many violent battles between the armies of Huascar and Atahualpa.

Now it seemed the amautas' prophecies, which had so terrified Huayna Capac, were coming true. The last part of those prophecies had been the most gloomy and most frightening. 'The Empire will disappear,' the amautas had warned. 'Foreigners will take it from us.' This too was going to come true.

In 1528 and 1529, while Huascar and Atahualpa were waging war against each other, Francisco Pizarro was in Spain. There, he persuaded King Charles to give permission for the exploration and conquest of Peru.

In January 1530, Pizarro left Spain and crossed the Atlantic Ocean to Panama. He spent a long time preparing his expedition, but at last at the end of 1531 (the exact date is uncertain), he set sail from Panama with three ships laden with men and horses. His destination was Tumbez, on the north-western coast of the Inca Empire.

By the time Pizarro and his expedition arrived at Tumbez, the Inca civil war was drawing to an end. Atahualpa had made his camp at Cajamarca, which lay on a plateau 10,000 feet (3,000 m) up in the Andes. Huascar, he knew, was nearby and he sent a force of some five thousand men to find him.

The unfortunate Huascar was marching along a small track accompanied by only seven hundred men when Atahualpa's soldiers swept down upon them. Huascar's tiny force had no chance against so many men. After a short, sharp fight, they turned and fled back towards Cuzco. Huascar was captured and taken to Atahualpa in Cajamarca.

The victorious Atahualpa threw Huascar into prison in the mountain fortress of Xuaca, some 300 miles (480 km) south of Cajamarca. He ordered all Huascar's sons and relatives and friends to be killed and proclaimed himself ruler of the whole Inca Empire.

In fact, Atahualpa was what we call a *usurper*, for he had stolen the throne of the Incas from its rightful owner, Huascar. All the same, the inhabitants of Cuzco and other parts of the Empire hailed Atahualpa as their new Sapa Inca. 'May the Sun grant him long life and happiness!' they cried.

As the new Sapa Inca, one of the first pieces of news Atahualpa received in Cajamarca was that 'white men with beards' who were 'masters of lightning' had arrived at Tumbez, 300 miles (480 km) away across the Andes, accompanied by 'great four-legged beasts'.

The 'white men with beards' were, of course, Pizarro and his expedition.

The 'lightning' was their cannons and muskets, and the 'great four-legged beasts' were Pizarro's horses.

From this description of the Spaniards, which a chasqui brought to Atahualpa, you might think that the Incas were a very simple, primitive people. In many ways they were. Obviously they knew little or nothing about guns, and few of them had ever seen a horse. In addition, they did not even know what a wheel was. Even so, it would be a great mistake to look on the Incas of Peru as nothing but barbarians or savages. In several ways, they were more advanced than the Spaniards or other Europeans of the time.

For instance, the Empire of the Incas was what we would today describe as a socialist 'welfare state', the sort of state that did not arise in Europe until our own century. In practice, this meant that no one could be very rich and no one could be very poor. The Inca government made sure that everyone had sufficient to eat, everyone had enough clothing to wear and everyone had a proper home.

Of course, there was a price to pay for all these benefits from the state. That price was personal freedom. The ordinary Inca had no chance of changing his job and getting a better one, so that he could earn more money. Instead he had to do whatever work the government decided he should do, and faithfully perform all his duties. At the same time, the government also had its duties towards the people: it had to ensure that everyone was treated fairly and got a fair share of everything.

How did the Incas achieve their 'welfare state'? The basis of their system was 'nationalisation', or state ownership of the most important things in the Empire. These were the land, which produced food, the gold, silver and other mines, and the herds of llamas, which provided transport among other things.

The Incas divided their land into three parts. All the maize and other crops and plants grown on one part went to the gods and their priests. The produce of the second section of land was for the government: out of this, the Inca nobles were supplied with food and so were government officials, Inca craftsmen and the army. Everything grown on the third part of Inca lands went to supply the ordinary people.

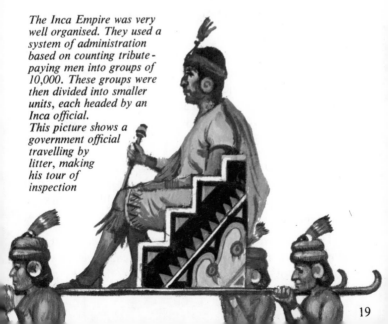

*The Inca Empire was very well organised. They used a system of administration based on counting tribute-paying men into groups of 10,000. These groups were then divided into smaller units, each headed by an Inca official.*
*This picture shows a government official travelling by litter, making his tour of inspection*

How much of the 'people's land' you got depended on the size of your family. A man and his wife got one *topo* of land (1 acre or 4,056 square metres). Each of their sons got an extra strip of land and each daughter half a strip.

Large areas of the Incas' farmlands were *terraced* (cut in steps into the mountainside). There were also many stone-lined irrigation channels, which brought water to the fields, sometimes from as far as 500 miles (804 km) away.

When the Inca family groups worked side by side in the fields, it was often a jolly, friendly business. They laughed and joked with one another as they worked on their strips of land and later when work was over, they might sit chatting and joking with one another and drinking pots of chicha beer, their favourite beverage.

If there was a particularly good harvest, the extra food that was produced was shared out equally among the people. If on the other hand a bad harvest, earthquake, storm or other calamity occurred, then the government gave food and grain from its storehouses to all who needed it.

These government storehouses also gave food to the old, to people who were crippled, blind or handicapped in any way, and to others who were unable to work on the land.

The food which the Incas ate was rather plain and simple, like most things in their lives. Meals usually consisted of boiled or roasted maize, potatoes and a grain called *quinoa*. Sometimes Inca housewives added a little meat or spices like hot chilis to give their dishes extra taste. In addition there was fish, various soups and stews, maize cakes and several different fruits and vegetables: these included avocado, manioc, beans, peanuts, bananas and guavas. A delicious treat was popcorn – that is, split roasted maize – cooked on clay stoves heated by sticks of burning wood.

*Farmers at work on terraced Inca farmlands. Deep stonelined irrigation channels brought water to the fields*

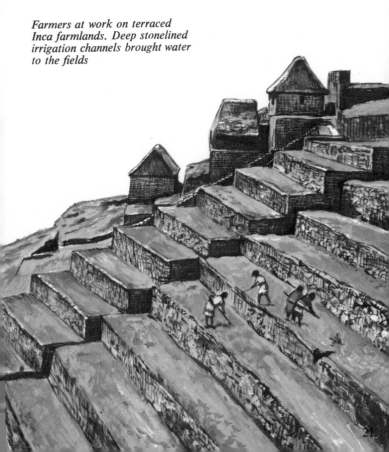

The Incas did not eat much meat because, until Europeans brought over great herds of beef cattle, there were not enough meat-bearing animals in South America. The little meat the Incas ate came mostly from guinea-pigs, which were delicious roasted, and from llamas. Llama meat tasted like mutton or lamb, but the Incas could not eat too much of it, for these large strong animals were important to their lives in other ways. They were needed not only for the transport they provided, they were also needed for their wool, as pack animals for carrying wool, cotton,

*A llama caravan carrying goods through the Andes*

metals and other goods, and as sacrifices at religious festivals.

The herds of llamas were divided up in much the same way as the land was. Most Inca farmers had no more than ten each. The largest number of llamas were the property of the government. Government llamas provided the people with wool for clothes. Each family received as much wool as it needed for its members. This was then taken home and woven into clothes on simple hand-looms.

Inca clothes were usually the simplest of garments. Both men and women wore cotton or llama wool tunics consisting of two rectangles of cloth sewn together, with holes left for the arms and head. No piece of clothing could be plainer than that, and people were discouraged from making grander garments for themselves. The reason was that if they were too splendidly dressed, they might get it into their heads that they were better than other people.

Yet in spite of this restriction, the Incas sometimes made their tunics look a bit special by dyeing them in brilliant hues, weaving them in interesting patterns, or giving them beautiful borders made from squares, triangles, diamonds and other shapes. Most magnificent

*An Inca woman weaving*

24

*Inca farmers working on the land*

of all was cloth woven with gold thread or decorated with small gold and silver ornaments.

Over their tunics, men and women wore cloaks to protect them from the mountain cold. Both men and women, too, wore sandals made from wool, aloe-fibre or llama hides.

Except when they were working on the land, the men wore fringes of wool around their knees and also round their ankles. They wore a lot of jewellery as well, much more than the women did. This was because jewellery to the Incas was a sign of a man's rank or importance.

*The festival of* Inti Raymi *began at dawn*

Members of the Inca royal family, for instance, wore 2-inch (5 cm) wide plugs of gold pushed through their ear lobes. Spanish historians frequently called them *Orejones* ('Big Ears') because the heavy plugs made their ears so large. If a man wore a large metal disc hanging from his neck, this showed that he was a warrior who had been decorated for bravery in battle.

This jewellery all sounds very splendid, but it was just ordinary everyday dress for important people in the Inca Empire. The real dressing-up time came during the frequent religious festivals. It was then that the men put on brilliantly coloured and patterned head-dresses, collars made of brightly coloured feathers, or painted their faces.

The Incas believed they had to look their most magnificent at religious ceremonies because it was very important for them to honour their gods and keep them in a good mood. This was also the reason why the Incas sacrificed llamas, and sometimes humans, to their gods.

Illapa and Viracocha were very important Inca gods, but the greatest of them all was Inti, the Sun. All life came from the Sun, the Incas believed, and of all the Inca religious festivals Inti Raymi – the Feast of the Sun – was the most magnificent.

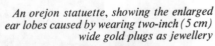

*An orejon statuette, showing the enlarged ear lobes caused by wearing two-inch (5 cm) wide gold plugs as jewellery*

27

In June, when the winter solstice occurred in South America and the sun began to move northwards towards the Equator, the hills around Cuzco were the scene of great festivities and celebrations. Young children who were to be sacrifices to Inti (and sometimes specially chosen women) were led round a huge idol of the god. This consisted of a golden disc with large rays spreading out from it. The children were afterwards buried alive together with gold and silver objects, llamas and ground sea shells. Afterwards there was a great banquet, and people danced and sang in the main square of the city.

Fortunately, humans were sacrificed only on very important festivals or at a Sapa Inca's coronation. More often, the Incas sacrificed llamas, guinea-pigs, gold and silver ornaments, small human-shaped wood carvings, and sometimes beads, shells

*Atahualpa arriving for the Feast of the Sun*

and feathers. They also offered food. Each day at the Coricancha, the Sun Temple in Cuzco, a wood fire, lit at sunrise, was sprinkled with food for the sun to eat; later in the day, priests sacrificed a dark red coloured llama which was then burned on a cocawood fire.

The priests who conducted the ceremonies, heard people confess their sins, and dealt with all the many tasks required by the Inca religion, were the most important group of people in the whole Empire. They were headed by the Villac Uma, the Highest Priest, who was second in rank only to the Sapa Inca himself. After the Villac Uma came the Hatun Uillca (bishops) and then the Yana Uillca, the mass of ordinary priests. There were also Inca priestesses, like the Chosen Women who served in the sun temples. Other priestesses were in charge of the shrine to Mother Moon (Mama-Quilla) and of the great solid silver disc which represented her. The Incas thought the Moon was the wife of the sun.

The Incas were very superstitious. If a shooting star appeared in the sky, they thought that was a bad sign, and so was the hooting of an owl. A fire that spluttered and gave off sparks was supposed by the Incas to be angry, so they poured a little chicha beer on it to calm it down.

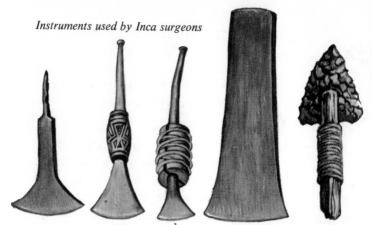

*Instruments used by Inca surgeons*

When the Incas fell ill, they relied on all sorts of superstitious practices to drive their sickness away. A sick person might try to cure himself by going to a point where two rivers joined and there rubbing himself all over with a mixture of maize and water. If an Inca broke a bone in his leg or arm or some other part of his body, he would go back to the place where the accident occurred. There he made sacrifices because it was believed that he had angered the god at that place and so made the god break the bone.

Sacrifices and rituals were not the only things the Incas used in times of illness or accident. They were also very skilful surgeons. They knew the art of *trepanning* the skull (cutting a piece out), which meant that they could mend fractures or help people suffering from brain disorders. They were also clever at *amputating* (cutting off) diseased limbs, and at burning out wounds to prevent infection. Before performing an operation, Inca surgeons used to give their patients drugs like coca to make them drowsy or send them to sleep. Or they made them drunk with chicha beer, or they hypnotised them. Inca surgeons also cleaned out their operating rooms by burning maize flour: this helped to kill germs that could cause infections. Sending patients to sleep with anaesthetics and disinfecting operating rooms was not widely practised in Europe until the nineteenth century, hundreds of years later.

*Present day ruins of the mighty fortress at Sacsahuaman*

Unlike most Europeans of their time, the Incas also realised that if you wanted to be healthy, then you had to be clean. The Inca government encouraged the ordinary Incas to believe that it was good and virtuous to wash often, and the Sapa Inca set a good example by taking regular baths.

The Sapa Inca used to wash himself in a sunken bath made from stone set in the grounds of his palace. It was filled with water through copper pipes or drains made of stone. When royal baths were built near natural hot springs, the royal bathwater was drawn from that.

Cajamarca had a hot spring, and in 1532 Atahualpa enjoyed many warm, relaxing baths while he was waiting for Pizarro and his companions to arrive.

The most magnificent and impressive structures erected by the Incas were their royal palaces, fortresses, temples and shrines. These large buildings were often made from huge square blocks of limestone or volcanic rock, each of which could be as much as 20 ft (6 m) long. However, the Incas also built fine towns where people lived in adobe-mud or stone houses grouped round wide courtyards. Inca architects were very careful about cleanliness both in homes and in the storehouses where food was kept. So they made sure that towns had good drains to carry away sewage and dirt, particularly in places where water might collect and form stagnant, unhealthy pools.

Important Inca towns were joined by a network of roads. These roads spread out to cover the whole Inca Empire and eventually covered 15,500 miles (25,000 km). The highways built through the mountains were about 3 ft (1 m) wide and where the land was rocky or steep, they would have steps cut into them. Where roads ran across marshes or streams, Inca engineers built *causeways* (stone platforms) to carry them.

*Peruvian Pottery*

Travelling in Peru was a very long, slow business because the fastest speed at which the Incas could travel was the speed of their best llamas. So the Incas built rest-houses called *tambos* and small food stores for travellers. The chasquis, who often ran 50 miles (80 km) in a single day, used roadside shelters, which were built at short regular intervals.

The most dangerous part of travelling in the Inca Empire came when deep mountain ravines had to be crossed. To span these ravines, rope bridges were formed from braided twisted fibres, vines or twigs. These bridges, which could sway alarmingly in a strong wind, were often very long. One Spaniard later wrote of how he crossed a bridge near Cuzco which spanned a ravine 200 ft (60 m) wide.

Naturally thousands of labourers were needed to build and repair bridges and roads and erect houses and other structures. For this purpose, men in the Inca Empire had to give a total of about five years' working time to the government when they were between the ages of 25 and 50.

Compulsory government service was called *mita*. In addition to working on building schemes, men could serve their mita time by labouring in the gold and silver mines or by joining the Inca army.

The Inca army was very well organised, and extremely disciplined. Inca soldiers who failed to march in proper order along the roads, or who stole from people in the regions through which they passed, could be punished with the death penalty.

*When the Inca army was on the move, it used supply dumps placed at intervals along the roads, where lodging houses were also built for soldiers to rest or spend the night*

Because they did not have to carry their supplies with them, Inca armies could move very swiftly and often attacked their enemies long before they were expected. Just before a battle was about to start, Inca soldiers began to sing very boastful songs at the tops of their voices, yelling at the enemy how brave and strong they were. Then they shouted terrible insults at the enemy and thumped on tambourine drums and played discordant music on flutes made of bone. All this was meant to frighten their foes, and so were the conch-shell and clay trumpets the Inca soldiers blew as signals to each other while the battle was being fought.

Since the hand weapons used by Inca warriors were mostly still fashioned in bronze or stone they were less effective than the steel weapons of the Spaniards. Inca soldiers used a variety of spears, darts, clubs and hand axes. Some of the smaller hand axes called champis (head breakers) had circular stone or bronze heads with star shaped spikes. They also used slings, belts of wool or fibre from which stones the size of an apple could be hurled with deadly force and accuracy

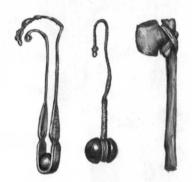

After the Incas had won a battle, they took a certain number of prisoners and paraded them through the streets of Cuzco. The rest of the defeated army was allowed to return home, but not before they were made to understand that they were now subjects of the mighty Sapa Inca. To make sure of this thousands of captives taken from a newly-vanquished tribe or province were made to lie flat on the ground in the Sun Temple at Cuzco while the Sapa Inca put his foot on their backs or necks.

*Statuette of a warrior in a style that was later copied by the Incas*

'On my enemies I step!' he cried.

Conquerors like the Incas were used to facing enemies. However, on November 15, 1532, they suddenly found themselves facing a new kind of enemy, who was much more cunning and brutal than any they had met before. Those enemies were Francisco Pizarro and his Spaniards, and November 15, 1532 was the day on which they arrived at last in Cajamarca after their exhausting mountain journey.

*After his capture, the Spaniards tried to convert Atahualpa to Christianity*

Of course, when the Spaniards arrived, the Incas did not realise they were enemies, but it was not very long before the Incas learned the terrible truth.

On the morning after the Spaniards' arrival, Atahualpa was carried in a litter into the town square at Cajamarca to meet Francisco Pizarro and twenty of his men, who were awaiting him there. Two thousand princes, singers and dancers preceded Atahualpa's litter, together with dozens of people who swept the road clear for the barefooted litter-bearers.

Pizarro and the Spaniards gasped at the magnificent sight of Atahualpa riding in his litter. The tall, handsome Sapa Inca sat proudly on the great gold throne, with glittering gold ornaments decorating his long, glossy black hair and a splendid collar round his neck made up of large emeralds.

Atahualpa's long robe stretched to his ankles and the litter was lined inside with the brilliantly coloured feathers of tropical birds. Shining out from among them were gold and silver discs.

As the litter bearers came to a halt in the centre of the square, Father Vincente de Valverde, a Spanish Catholic priest, approached Atahualpa and told him: 'We are here in the name of Jesus Christ and of our great king, Charles of Spain. We demand that you now become Christians like ourselves, and accept King Charles as your ruler.'

Valverde held up a Bible. 'This book,' he told Atahualpa, 'tells the story of our great Christian religion!'

When Valverde's words were translated to him,
Atahualpa frowned and his lips trembled with anger.
No one had ever dared to speak to him like this before.
Even so, Atahualpa was curious. Valverde's Bible was
probably the first book he had ever seen. He took it
from Valverde's hand and turned the pages. Then he
put it to his ear and listened, looking angrier than ever.

'This book tells me nothing!' he cried. 'I cannot
hear it speak!'

With that, Atahualpa threw the Bible to the ground.
The Spaniards gasped at this frightful insult to their
holy book and Valverde's face turned red with fury.
Francisco Pizarro, who was nearby,
waved a white scarf as a signal to the
Spaniards standing by a large gun

which they had concealed close to the square. With a great thundering boom, the gun fired a shot. Then one of Pizarro's men raised a trumpet to his lips and blew a long, loud note.

'Santiago! Santiago!' yelled the Spaniards and with this battle cry, they drew their swords and rushed towards the Incas. The unarmed Incas were helpless as the Spaniards stabbed and slashed at them. At the sound of the trumpet, which was another signal, more Spaniards, armed with swords and muskets, ran into the square from their hiding-places in the surrounding streets. Others rode in on their horses to join the fight. Soon dozens of Incas lay on the ground dead or injured, and the air was filled with screams and shouts and yells.

Dozens of princes were killed trying to protect Atahualpa. Atahualpa's life was saved by Pizarro himself. Just as a Spaniard was raising his sword to strike the Sapa Inca, Pizarro yelled out: 'The Inca king is my own prisoner! I want him alive!'

Pizarro rushed up, grabbed Atahualpa by the hair and pulled him out of the litter. As Atahualpa sprawled on the ground, the Spaniards jumped on him, bound his hands and carried him to a nearby house.

*Atahualpa being snatched from his litter by Pizarro*

When night fell over Cajamarca, three or four thousand Incas lay dead in and around the square and Atahualpa was Pizarro's prisoner.

Atahualpa was a clever man, and within a few days he had learned enough Spanish to understand what his captors were talking about. The things the Spaniards talked about most were gold, silver and jewels. So Atahualpa thought of a plan to win back his freedom.

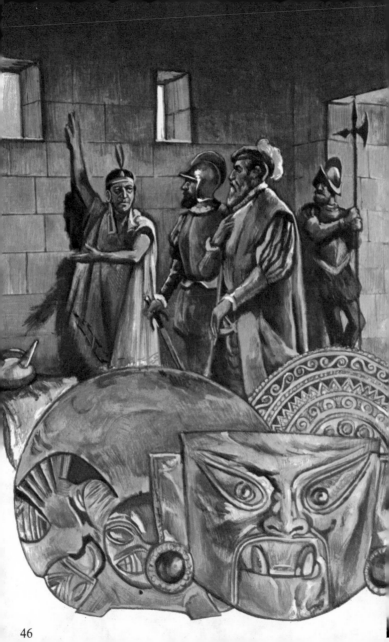

'I will pay you a huge ransom,' he told Pizarro. 'I will order my people to fill a room full of gold and a room full of silver to pay the ransom.' Pizarro quickly agreed. He knew the Incas did whatever their Sapa Inca told them. He also knew that Peru contained enough gold and silver to fill several rooms several times over.

Chasquis were sent speeding out all over the Empire with Atahualpa's orders and the people began to gather gold and silver to pay this enormous ransom. They stripped temple walls of ornaments, and took all the gold and silver out of shrines and palaces. All this was sent to Cajamarca and the 'gold' and 'silver' rooms soon began to fill up.

When at last all the ransom had been collected, it amounted to over three million pounds' worth of gold and about twelve tonnes of silver.

Most of it was melted down and divided out among the Spaniards. Francisco Pizarro got the biggest share – over half a million pounds – and he also took Atahualpa's magnificent gold throne, which was worth another £250,000.

Now the ransom had been paid, Atahualpa naturally expected the Spaniards to free him. The Spaniards, however, were afraid that if they did this, Atahualpa would order his subjects to attack them and drive them out of Peru. This was why the Spaniards decided that Atahualpa had to die.

While he had been a captive, Atahualpa had given secret orders for the killing of his half-brother Huascar and these orders had been carried out. This gave the Spaniards an excuse to put Atahualpa on trial.

'You have committed murder!' they accused him. 'You must be punished! And our punishment for murder is death!'

Atahualpa was amazed and horrified. He had never imagined that the Spaniards would break their word and fail to free him. When he heard the punishment he was to suffer, he wept bitterly and implored the Spaniards to spare his life. It was no use: the Spaniards would not change their minds.

They did however say that if Atahualpa became a Christian he would not be burned to death, as non-Christians and heretics were.

After nightfall on August 29, 1533, Atahualpa was led out into the square at Cajamarca, which was lit by flaming torches. Father Valverde baptised him as a Christian and then, after he had begged Pizarro to take care of his children, Atahualpa was strangled to death.

In this tragic way, the last great Sapa Inca of Peru ended his life and with that, the Inca Empire also came to an end.

Afterwards, the Spaniards occupied Peru and it later became one of their many colonies in the South American continent. They ruled the former Inca Empire–and ruled it cruelly–for nearly three centuries, until 1824, when Peru became an independent country once again.

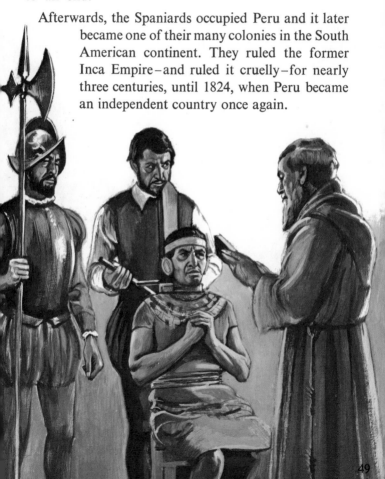

By that time of course it had changed completely from the land the sixteenth century Incas had known. All the same, the Incas had not completely disappeared. Even today, you can see many Peruvians whose faces are almost exactly the same as those of Atahualpa's subjects, and who speak Quechua, a language not very different from the one they spoke four hundred years ago. If you go up into the Andes, far away from Lima and other big modern cities, you can still see people

*The Inca city of Machu Picchu, which Pizarro's men never discovered*

working in the fields, just as their ancestors once worked for the government of the far-flung Inca Empire. You can still see Inca towns, like Machu Picchu, on their high mountain plateaux. Surrounded by a great ring of craggy mountain peaks, these towns have not changed much from the time when the ancient Incas lived there and ran their 'welfare state', obeyed their Sapa Inca and worshipped the Sun.

# INDEX